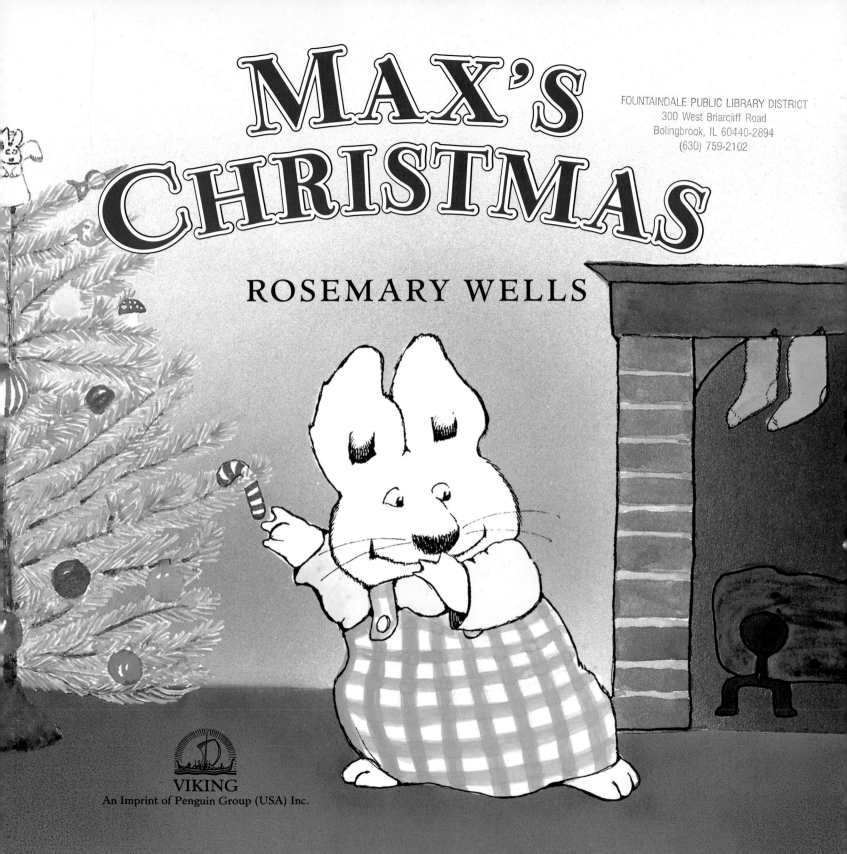

MAX'S CHRISTMAS

ROSEMARY WELLS

VIKING
An Imprint of Penguin Group (USA) Inc.

For Beezoo Wells

VIKING
Published by Penguin Group
Penguin Young Readers Group, 345 Hudson Street, New York, New York 10014, U.S.A.
Penguin Group (Canada), 90 Eglinton Avenue East, Suite 700, Toronto, Ontario, Canada M4P 2Y3
(a division of Pearson Penguin Canada Inc.)
Penguin Books Ltd, 80 Strand, London WC2R 0RL, England
Penguin Ireland, 25 St Stephen's Green, Dublin 2, Ireland (a division of Penguin Books Ltd)
Penguin Group (Australia), 250 Camberwell Road, Camberwell, Victoria 3124, Australia
(a division of Pearson Australia Group Pty Ltd)
Penguin Books India Pvt Ltd, 11 Community Centre, Panchsheel Park, New Delhi – 110 017, India
Penguin Group (NZ), 67 Apollo Drive, Rosedale, North Shore 0632, New Zealand
(a division of Pearson New Zealand Ltd.)
Penguin Books (South Africa) (Pty) Ltd, 24 Sturdee Avenue, Rosebank, Johannesburg 2196, South Africa

Penguin Books Ltd, Registered Offices: 80 Strand, London WC2R 0RL, England

First published by Dial Books for Young Readers in 1986
This edition published in 2010 by Viking, a division of Penguin Young Readers Group

1 3 5 7 9 10 8 6 4 2

The Library of Congress has cataloged the original edition as follows:
Wells, Rosemary. Max's Christmas.
Summary: Max waits up on Christmas Eve to see Santa Claus coming down the chimney.
[1. Christmas—Fiction. 2. Santa Claus—Fiction. 3. Rabbits—Fiction.] 1. Title.
PZ7.W46843Masg 1986 [E] 85-27547
ISBN 0-8037-0290-6

This edition ISBN: 978-0-670-88715-6

Manufactured in China
Set in Minister

"Guess what, Max!"
said Max's sister, Ruby.
"What?" said Max.

"It's Christmas Eve, Max," said Ruby,
"and you know who's coming?"
"Who?" said Max.

"Santa Claus is coming,
that's who," said Ruby.
"When?" said Max.

"Tonight, Max, he's coming tonight!"
said Ruby.
"Where?" said Max.
"Spit, Max," said Ruby.

"Santa Claus is coming right down
our chimney into our living room,"
said Ruby.
"How?" said Max.

"That's enough questions, Max.

You have to go to sleep fast,
before Santa Claus comes," said Ruby.

But Max wanted to stay up
to see Santa Claus.
"No, Max," said Ruby.

"Nobody ever sees Santa Claus."
"Why?" said Max.
"BECAUSE!" said Ruby.

But Max didn't believe a word
Ruby said.

So he sneaked downstairs . . .

and waited for Santa Claus.

Max waited a long time.

Suddenly, ZOOM! Santa
jumped down the chimney
into the living room.

"Don't look, Max!" said Santa Claus.
"Why?" said Max.
"Because," said Santa Claus,
"nobody is supposed to see me!"

"Why?" said Max.
"Because everyone is supposed to be asleep in bed," said Santa Claus.

But Max peeked at Santa anyway.
"Guess what, Max!" said Santa Claus.
"What?" said Max.

"It's time for me to go away
and you to go to sleep,"
said Santa Claus.
"Why?" said Max.

"BECAUSE!" said Santa Claus.

Ruby came downstairs.
"What happened, Max?" asked Ruby.
"Who were you talking to?
Where did you get that hat?

Max! Why is your blanket
so humpy and bulgy?"

"BECAUSE!" said Max.